# Armadillo Antics

# Bill Martin Jr
# and Michael Sampson

## Illustrated by Nathalie Beauvois

BROWN BOOKS KIDS

© 2022 Michael Sampson

This is a work of fiction. Any similarity to real persons, living or dead,
is coincidental and not intended by the author.

# Armadillo Antics

Brown Books Kids
Dallas / New York
www.BrownBooksKids.com
(972) 381-0009

A New Era in Publishing®

Publisher's Cataloging-In-Publication Data

Names: Martin, Bill, 1916-2004, author. | Sampson, Michael R., author. | Beauvois, Nathalie, illustrator.
Title: Armadillo antics / Bill Martin Jr. and Michael Sampson ; illustrated by Nathalie Beauvois.
Description: Dallas ; New York : Brown Books Kids, [2022] | Interest age level: 005-006. | Summary:
    Follow an adventurous armadillo through nighttime fun as dawn approaches.
Identifiers: ISBN 9781612545479 (hardcover)
Subjects: LCSH: Armadillos--Juvenile fiction. | Play--Juvenile fiction. | Night--Juvenile fiction. | CYAC:
    Armadillos--Fiction. | Play--Fiction. | Night--Fiction.
Classification: LCC PZ8.3.M418 Ar 2022 | DDC [E]--dc23

This book has been officially leveled by using the
F&P Text Level Gradient™ Leveling System.

ISBN 978-1-61254-547-9
LCCN 2021948735

Printed in China
10 9 8 7 6 5 4 3 2 1

For more information or to contact the author, please go to
www.BrownBooksKids.com.

MS—To Rowan Sampson

NB—To Paula and Pedro

Now the day has ended,
and the birds no longer fly.
Shadows of the evening
dance across the sky.

As the full moon rises,
and the frogs begin to leap,
the creatures of the wild
soon will be asleep.

All except the armadillo,
on the prowl

at the sound of the timber wolf's mournful howl.

Armadillo,

Armadillo,

Armadillo, run.

**Romp and play
till the night is done.**

Armadillo,

Armadillo,

Armadillo, grin.

**Your little brother
looks like your twin.**

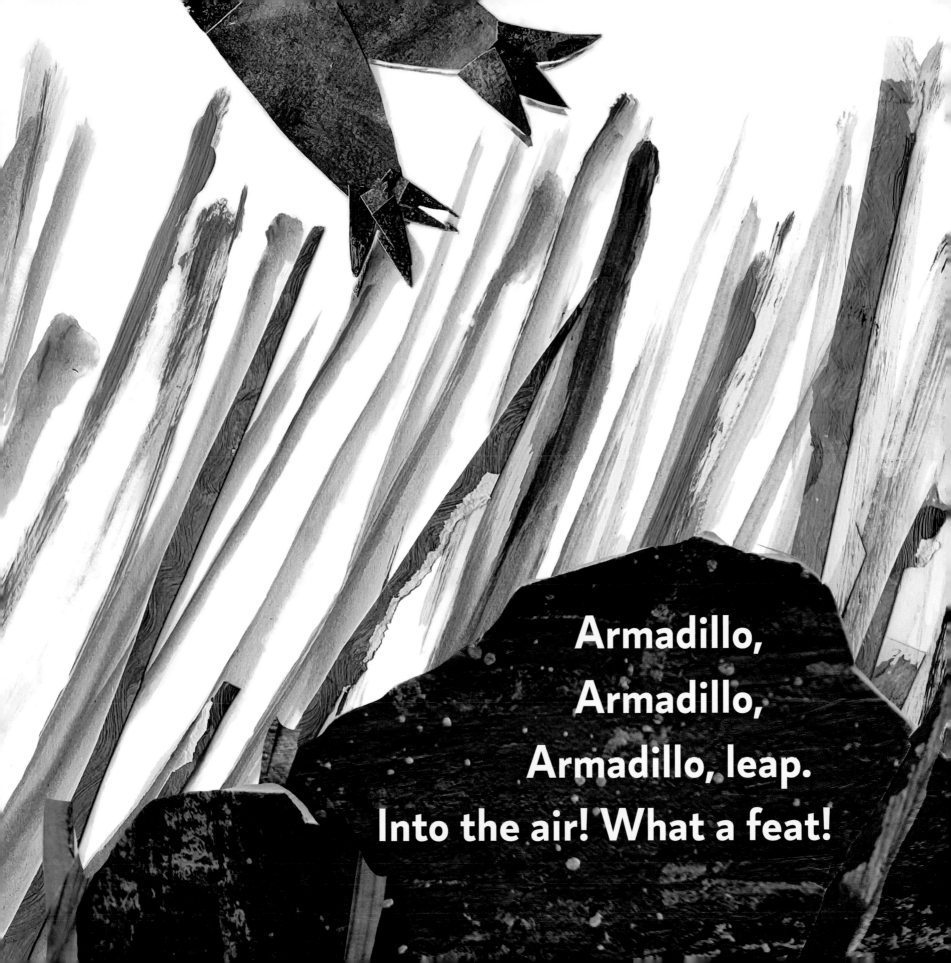

Armadillo,
Armadillo,
Armadillo, leap.
Into the air! What a feat!

Armadillo,

Armadillo,

Armadillo, run.

Escape from the dog
and have some fun.

Armadillo, Armadillo,

Armadillo, dig

into your burrow,

then dance a jig.

Armadillo, Armadillo, Armadillo, look,

or you may fall into the brook.

Armadillo,

Armadillo,

Armadillo,

**MIGHT,**

dressed in armor
like a knight.

Armadillo,

Armadillo,

Armadillo, flee.

You've just met an
ANGRY BEE!

**Armadillo, Armadillo,
Armadillo, eat.**

Roots and grubs—
what a treat!

**Armadillo, Armadillo, Armadillo, run,**

or you'll never
see the rising sun.

Armadillo, Armadillo, Armadillo, rest.

Have sweet dreams inside your nest.

# Armadillo Facts

The armadillo is nocturnal, sleeping during the day and awake during the night.

The armadillo is protected by bone-like material called armor, from which it gets its name.

The armadillo has two major enemies— dogs and cars.

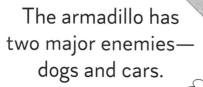

The snout of the armadillo is as strong as steel.

The armadillo is nearsighted and almost blind.

The armadillo can run ten miles an hour.

The armadillo can jump up to ten times its height.

The armadillo has a very healthy diet—yuk, roots, and grub worms.